DIGGING YOUR OWN GRAVE

By B. L. Andrews

with illustrations by Arnold Roth

St. Martin's Press   New York

DIGGING YOUR OWN GRAVE

Copyright © 1994 by B. L. Andrews.
Illustrations copyright © 1994 by Arnold Roth.

All rights reserved. No part of this book may be used or reproduced in any manner whatsoever without written permission except in the case of brief quotations embodied in critical articles or reviews. For information, write to St. Martin's Press, 175 Fifth Avenue, New York, N.Y. 10010.

ISBN: 0-312-95358-5

Printed in the United States of America

St. Martin's Paperbacks edition / August 1994

10 9 8 7 6 5 4 3 2 1

INTRODUCTION

I have always been amazed that the human race has survived as a species. From the moment a child is born it seems to be motivated towards destruction. Babies will eat battery acid, if that's all they can find. And by the time a human has entered the teenage years it is as though there is a conscious desire to do what is most destructive to the continuation of life. Adulthood is too painful to even discuss.

Did the dinosaurs also make some unfortunate life choices that hastened their extinction? Perhaps they went meat-eating in a vegetarian world. Maybe they voted Republican. It's hard to say.

I, for one, would like to see us survive. Perhaps this book will remind people that life is fragile, that we are the caretakers of our own existence, and that almost anyone can publish a book. Let me know what you think.

B. L. Andrews

1. ❖ Stand between Oprah and a buffet table.

2. ❖ Go for a midnight drive with Ted Kennedy.

3. ❖ Tell the emergency-room doctor that you're an organ donor.

4. ❖ Accompany Salman Rushdie on his next author tour.

5. ❖ Eat at a Jack-in-the-Box and order your hamburger over-easy.

6. ❖ Vote Democratic in the next election.

7. ❖ Vote Republican in the next election.

8. ❖ Take a job as a supervisor with the U.S. Postal Service.

9. ❖ Go to a park in New York City wearing a Rolex and a gold chain, riding a brand-new mountain bike.

10. ❖ Ask a woman if she's pregnant when she's not.

11. ❖ Hitchhike with a sign that says "No relatives and no one knows where I am."

12. ❖ Get an English degree in college as your economic base for the future.

13. ❖ Because you can't get a job right out of college, go back to school to get your Masters degree in English.

14. ❖ Make an appointment with Dr. Kevor-kian for your next annual physical.

15. ❖ Book a flight on a DC-10.

16. ❖ Invest your life savings in Ethiopian agriculture.

17. ❖ Drive through downtown Miami with-out having removed the rental sticker from the license plate of the car.

18. ❖ Tell a feminist that what she really needs is a man to slap some sense into her.

19. ❖ Get a blood transfusion in a New York City hospital.

20. ❖ Wear a dry-cleaning bag and a rubber band for your costume next Halloween.

21. ❖ Charter the boat "Golden Venture" for your return trip back to the U.S. from China.

22. ❖ Pray at a Muslim temple in Serbia.

23. ❖ Become a parking-lot attendant at the World Trade Center.

24. ❖ Tell a group of drinking Marine buddies that you joined the service because you're looking for a few good men.

25. ❖ If you're a woman, just be in the same room with a group of drinking Marines.

26. ❖ Go roller-blading blindfolded in San Francisco.

27. ❖ Demand five dollars from Bernie Goetz.

28. ❖ Eat rice cakes with beer.

29. ❖ Accept a ride home from school from someone who says they are a good friend of the family.

30. ❖ Go on a water-tasting trip through India.

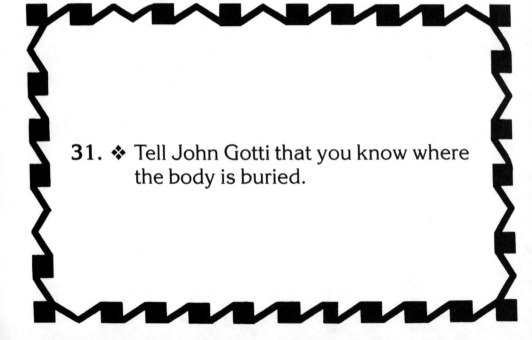

31. ❖ Tell John Gotti that you know where the body is buried.

32. ❖ Go hunting wearing a fur coat.

33. ❖ Wear a t-shirt on a Miami beach that says "Castro for President."

34. ❖ Get nominated for a position in the Clinton Administration.

35. ❖ Take a hot-air balloon ride over Washington, D.C.

36. ❖ Get a political endorsement from Al Sharpton.

37. ❖ Swim in the Hudson River with your mouth open.

38. ❖ See how many extra days you can get out of your razor.

39. ❖ Emulate Madonna.

40. ❖ Open up your heart and believe everything your lover tells you.

41. ❖ Get a tan under the ozone hole.

42. ❖ Volunteer to confront the company boss with employee demands.

43. ❖ Be a subject for cosmetic industry testing.

44. ❖ Travel alone in Iran wearing short-shorts, no bra, and a tank top.

45. ❖ Move to the Midwest.

46. ❖ Go on a Kool-Aid liquid diet.

47. ❖ Get silicone breast implants.

48. ❖ Tease a pit bull.

49. ❖ Crawl into the polar bear exhibit at the zoo with a bag of garbage.

50. ❖ Watch an afternoon of televised golf because you need to stay awake.

51. ❖ Believe in the superiority of American cars.

52. ❖ Hang out in South LA wearing a "Rodney King Was Guilty" t-shirt.

53. ❖ Underestimate the length of your Bungee cord.

54. ❖ Live in a trailer park.

55. ❖ Go back to college when you're forty and live in a dorm.

56. ❖ Take a paparazzi photo of Sean Penn.

57. ❖ Go inner-tubing off the coast of Cuba.

58. ❖ Polish your silverware with mercury.

59. ❖ Adopt a troubled, emotionally scarred teenage boy who collects knives and worships the devil.

60. ❖ Play musical chairs in San Quentin.

61. ❖ Eat at Taco Bell and then stand near an open flame.

62. ❖ Walk through a hog farm with a truffle in your pants pocket.

63. ❖ Bend over in a prison shower.

64. ❖ Order sushi at a rural diner.

65. ❖ Decide not to stop when a cop tries to pull you over.

66. ❖ Give your boyfriend an ultimatum to choose between you and televised sports.

67. ❖ Watch a full episode of "Barney, the Dinosaur" with a pistol nearby.

68. ❖ Sit on a toilet seat in a New Jersey Turnpike restroom.

69. ❖ Rely on crystals to cure a serious illness.

70. ❖ Sleep with a sumo wrestler when it's his turn to be on top.

71. ❖ Rear-end a Ford that has a full tank of gas.

72. ❖ Get a nicotine patch and still smoke a full pack of cigarettes a day.

73. ❖ Go to an Irish soccer game and sit in the cheap seats.

74. ❖ Work in the same office as someone you once slept with.

75. ❖ Convince yourself that hip-huggers, bell-bottoms, and platform shoes make you more attractive.

76. ❖ Move back in with your parents.

77. ❖ Tell an Israeli that you're a Palestinian nationalist.

78. ❖ Tell your boss that you should have his job because you're smarter.

79. ❖ Vote to approve a toxic-waste dump in your town because you believe it will create more jobs.

80. ❖ Be totally honest in your love re-lationship.

81. ❖ Call a 900 number because you think you won something.

82. ❖ Join a religious cult because of its charismatic leader.

83. ❖ Publicly insult the Reverend Moon, Scientology, or the Gambino family.

84. ❖ Spend an evening at the Kennedy compound without taking a reliable witness.

85. ❖ Launch your acting career on a sit-com spin-off show.

86. ❖ Volunteer to be a guest on "The Howard Stern Show."

87. ❖ Eat at a Polynesian-style restaurant.

88. ❖ Believe that psychoanalysis is worth the money.

89. ❖ Ask a cab driver for the quickest way to get to your destination.

90. ❖ Fall in love with a married man with the belief that he'll leave his wife.

91. ❖ Ask Woody Allen if he'll babysit your children.

92. ❖ Give a politician the benefit of a doubt.

93. ❖ Buy a condominium hoping to turn a profit.

94. ❖ Get a tattoo of your lover's name.

95. ❖ Sing rap music when you're white.

96. ❖ Play the lottery as the best hope for the future.

97. ❖ Actually elect Ross Perot to any public office.

98. ❖ Send your young son alone on a camping trip with a priest.

99. ❖ Sign a pre-nuptial agreement.

100. ❖ Try to reason with a five-year-old child.

101. ❖ Go skinnydipping in the Amazon River.

102. ❖ Exchange your dollars to buy rubles.

103. ❖ Open a tanning salon in Nevada.

104. ❖ Don't save receipts because the odds are that the IRS will never audit your taxes.

105. ❖ Try on a bathing suit in front of the mirror under a fluorescent light during the middle of the winter.

106. ❖ Remain in your hometown after graduating from high school.

107. ❖ Buy a house downstream from a paper mill.

108. ❖ Volunteer to water someone's plants while they're gone.

109. ❖ Go on a blind date with someone who is only described as "having a really good sense of humor."

110. ❖ Tell your boyfriend that unfortunately size really does matter.

111. ❖ After being rude to the waiter, order your food extra-spicy in a Thai restaurant.

112. ❖ Answer a "personals" ad in *Soldier of Fortune* magazine.

113. ❖ Go barefoot on a New Jersey beach.

114. ❖ Try to smoke a cigarette in a California restaurant.

115. ❖ Check the "Yes" box on a mail-order piece to receive new product information.

116. ❖ Agree to chaperon a group of teenagers on a camping trip.

❖ B. L. ANDREWS ❖

117. ❖ Wear a pair of new shoes to a convention.

118. ❖ Buy a juicer, a yogurt-maker, a crock-pot, a fondue set, and a fruit/vegetable drying machine.

119. ❖ Go to Michael Jackson's plastic surgeon for a nose job.

120. ❖ Indicate "Poet" as your last job on a résumé.

121. ❖ Become emotionally attached to a goldfish, a hamster, or a baby turtle.

122. ❖ Tell your spouse that you had an affair because you really felt it would strengthen the marriage.

123. ❖ Confide in someone who does publicity for a living.

124. ❖ Quit drinking, smoking, and go on a diet at the same time.

125. ❖ Yell fire in an after-hours nightclub.

126. ❖ Go through customs carrying a rock musician's bag.

127. ❖ Invite the guys over for Super Bowl Sunday when you don't have a television set.

128. ❖ Insult a wealthy, old, sick relative.

129. ❖ Give up your job to become a consultant.

130. ❖ Take a cross-country bus trip.

131. ❖ Stare into the sun to watch an eclipse.

132. ❖ Sit next to a family with young children at the movie theater.

133. ❖ Try to bond with your child by accompanying him to a heavy-metal rock concert.

134. ❖ Substitute teach.

135. ❖ Drive a school bus.

136. ❖ Listen to a meditation tape while driving.

137. ❖ Confuse Mensa with Menses when hiring someone for a think tank.

138. ❖ Play Scrabble with a dyslexic.

139. ❖ Read Russian literature when you're depressed.

140. ❖ Offer to hold a nervous Arab's suit-case on an airplane.

141. ❖ Hit a Killer Beehive with a football.

142. ❖ Win the Lottery one week before your divorce settlement.

143. ❖ Remove a champagne cork with your teeth.

144. ❖ Try to impress the French with your wit.

145. ❖ Go on a hunger strike until the government balances the budget.

146. ❖ Drive a snowmobile across a frozen lake.

147. ❖ Learn to play the accordion to impress your girlfriend.

148. ❖ Play the electric guitar while taking a bath.

149. ❖ Attend a science-fiction convention to get fashion tips.

150. ❖ Hunt grizzly bears with only your cunning and a bow and arrow.

151. ❖ Offer earthquake insurance in California.

152. ❖ Take a job for the late shift in an all-night convenience store.

153. ❖ Get your medical degree in Grenada.

154. ❖ Use tweezers to clean the hair out of your nose.

155. ❖ Answer a help-wanted ad for a crash-dummy tester.

156. ❖ Have faith that the scientific community would not use genetic research for foul purposes.

157. ❖ Hire an anorexic cook for your restaurant.

158. ❖ Buy clothes that fit tight because you expect to lose weight.

159. ❖ Believe a shoe salesperson that says that the leather will stretch.

160. ❖ Give advice to a friend who is going through difficult times with a lover.

161. ❖ Buy a child a pet because they promise to take care of it.

162. ❖ Buy a child a pet that has a short life expectancy.

163. ❖ Buy a child a pet that has a long life expectancy.

164. ❖ Take a compatibility test with your spouse.

165. ❖ Accept a double-dog dare.

166. ❖ Join the Navy to see the world.

167. ❖ Give lingerie to an employee on Secretary's Day.

168. ❖ Wear a toupee.

169. ❖ Try to analyze a relationship.

170. ❖ Follow your own advice.

171. ❖ Ask someone what they really think of your new haircut.

172. ❖ Open the mail for a genetic scientist.

173. ❖ Go to a wedding reception where they serve no liquor.

174. ❖ Try to outsmart a two-year-old child.

175. ❖ Elope.

176. ❖ Accept a date with someone you met at the unemployment office.

177. ❖ Grow lima beans as your primary cash crop.

178. ❖ Get a tooth drilled at a dental school.

179. ❖ Pick wild mushrooms for a fresh salad.

❖ B. L. Andrews ❖

180. ❖ Use a public defender at your trial.

181. ❖ Buy a used computer because the new technology seems so far away.

182. ❖ Hire an illegal alien to clean your house while you run for office.

183. ❖ Go to a movie after having read the book.

184. ❖ Open the door when a religious zealot is canvassing the neighborhood.

185. ❖ Rent a porno film from a video store in a neighborhood where everyone knows you.

186. ❖ Actually invite a salesperson into your home to outline your insurance needs.

187. ❖ Take a dose of allergy medicine and then rev up the power saw to fell a tree.

188. ❖ Stick rented videos under the front car seat with the intention of re-turning them soon.

189. ❖ Wear white linen to a barbecue.

190. ❖ Advise a teenager to use her own judgment.

191. ❖ Encourage your son to date your boss's daughter.

192. ❖ Take small children out to dinner in a fancy restaurant.

193. ❖ Sit next to an Amway salesman on a cross-country flight.

194. ❖ Figure that you can make it just one more exit before stopping for gas.

195. ❖ Play "Truth Or Dare" with Evel Knievel.

196. ❖ Go to the beach for a quiet getaway on a Fourth-of-July weekend.

197. ❖ Eat at any restaurant whose name begins with "Chez."

198. ❖ Pick up a mountain lion cub because you don't see the mother around.

199. ❖ Wear a string bikini to the beach with a jealous boyfriend.

200. ❖ Pull a squirt gun on a Los Angeles cop for a joke.

201. ❖ Mistake a tick for a beneficial insect in your organic garden.

202. ❖ Invite Jesse Helms to a stag party.

203. ❖ Solicit a promotional blurb from Tipper Gore for a rap album.

204. ❖ Drive a Japanese import car to an executive interview at the Chrysler Corporation.

205. ❖ Dive for pennies in a rock quarry.

206. ❖ Brag about successes to siblings at a family get-together.

207. ❖ Teach a sensitivity class at Folsom Prison.

❖ B. L. ANDREWS ❖

208. ❖ Teach your dog how to eat from your plate at the
dinner table.

209. ❖ Believe that a pet bird and a pet cat can have an affectionate relationship because you love them both.

210. ❖ Take a paper route delivering the Sunday edition of *The New York Times*.

211. ❖ Talk to your boyfriend's ex-wife to gain some insight into the relationship.

212. ❖ Take work home every weekend because you believe it will be appreciated.

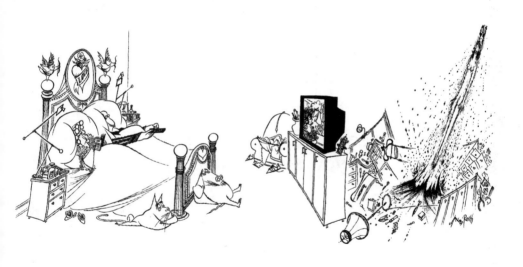

213. ❖ Set your vibrator on High.

214. ❖ Buy shoes or underwear at a garage sale.

215. ❖ Wear an asbestos oven mitt to protect yourself against burns.

216. ❖ Go for quantity rather than quality when choosing a fattening dessert.

217. ❖ Carry chocolate-covered marsh-mallows and a tuna-with-mayonnaise sandwich in your backpack for a hike on a hot summer day.

218. ❖ Say to your hairdresser "Surprise me."

219. ❖ Put a cigarette out on the side of an inflatable raft.

220. ❖ Give in to an incredible urge to "let it all hang out" in a public place.

221. ❖ Wear a water-resistant watch anywhere near moisture.

222. ❖ Take child-rearing advice from a Yuppie parent.

223. ❖ Hire a Hasidic group to build your barn and the Amish to appraise your jewelry.

224. ❖ Do a hilarious impression of your boss without first checking to see who's standing behind you.

225. ❖ Plant a little patch of kudzu in the garden.

226. ❖ Pass a winning lottery ticket around the bar for everyone to see.

227. ❖ Use a fake job offer as a bargaining chip to get a promotion.

228. ❖ Wear a fur hat and leather to an animal rights rally.

229. ❖ Eat something you can't identify from a carton in the refrigerator.

230. ❖ Ask a proud new father if he has any photos of the baby.

231. ❖ Walk against the light because pedestrians are supposed to have the right of way.

232. ❖ Leave a blank check with a car mechanic.

233. ❖ Clip a cat's nails while giving it a bath.

234. ❖ Give your in-laws a portable phone for Christmas.

235. ❖ Try to calm your nerves by playing a video game.

236. ❖ Go on an overseas trip with someone you just met.

237. ❖ Try to fool the public by combing
your hair up over a bald spot.

238. ❖ Strike up a meaningful conver-
sation with anyone in the music
business.

239. ❖ Spend a relaxing evening with a cocaine addict.

240. ❖ Take the advice of a guidance counselor.

241. ❖ Try to pick up someone in a bar by quoting Proust.

242. ❖ Tell a reporter from the *National Enquirer* that this is "off the record."

243. ❖ When asked to explain a tax discrepancy, tell the IRS that you don't believe in keeping records.

244. ❖ Buy the merchandising rights to a Robert Altman film.

245. ❖ Compete with Amy Fisher for a man.

246. ❖ Visit a friend that has recently purchased a photo CD system.

247. ❖ Name a previous boss who fired you as a reference.

248. ❖ Throw away an old comic book collection that has been stored in the attic since you were a kid.

249. ❖ Give a minor appliance to a girlfriend on Valentine's Day.

250. ❖ Ask directions from a Southern farmer when in a hurry.

251. ❖ Dye your blond hair black or your black hair blond.

252. ❖ Eat something that "tastes just like chicken."

253. ❖ Buy from a sperm bank located in the county where the movie *Deliverance* was made.

254. ❖ Get into an elevator with someone who is singing along with their Walkman.

255. ❖ Shallow-dive in the wading pool while the lifeguard isn't looking.

256. ❖ Wear contacts during a sandstorm.

257. ❖ Be last in line for the toilet on a return trip from Mexico.

258. ❖ Ask a man about his relationship with his father.

259. ❖ Buy a do-it-yourself kit that has an instruction booklet translated to English by the Japanese.

260. ❖ Anger a proctologist just before an exam.

261. ❖ Look to the British for social, political, or economic brilliance.

262. ❖ Pose for pornographic photos for fun because no one will ever find out.

263. ❖ Do a count of all the sexual partners you have had in your entire life.

264. ❖ Discipline someone else's naughty child.

265. ❖ Attempt to hop a Maglev train.

266. ❖ Try to foil an armed robbery by threatening to tell.

267. ❖ Play Frisbee on a penthouse balcony.

268. ❖ Petition the Pope for advice on women's issues.

269. ❖ Bring slapstick humor into the bedroom.

270. ❖ Marry a really good divorce lawyer.

271. ❖ Follow the circus parade barefooted.

272. ❖ Let someone with dentures take a bite out of your apple.

273. ❖ Eat an Italian sausage sandwich at the park just before jumping onto the triple-loop roller coaster.

274. ❖ Dry off your wet little dog in the microwave.

275. ❖ Try to prove your manhood to a group of other men.

276. ❖ Pry a stuck bagel out of the toaster with a metal fork.

277. ❖ Park a car with an alarm system in a nice quiet neighborhood.

278. ❖ Send to Eastern Europe for a piece of technical equipment.

279. ❖ Try to make a social statement by teaching in an inner-city school without a gun.

280. ❖ Buy prepared deli foods in a health food store.

281. ❖ Ask Carrie to the prom.

282. ❖ Sign a contract that only an attorney can understand.

283. ❖ Leave your home phone number with the office in case something comes up.

284. ❖ Fall asleep during a lover's quarrel.

285. ❖ Eat a snow cone to make yourself feel better after having a tooth drilled.

286. ❖ Wear a long flowing scarf around your neck for a ride in a convertible.

287. ❖ Recite Rod McKuen at a poetry slam.

288. ❖ Forget to pick up the bride's dress on her wedding day.

289. ❖ Instead of candy, give out good strong advice to a rowdy gang of teenagers on Halloween.

290. ❖ Raise your hand to ask a question at an auction.

291. ❖ Wear a sheer, clinging blouse to court to testify in your sexual harassment suit.

292. ❖ Offer to pick up the check BEFORE someone chooses a restaurant.

293. ❖ Pop a cube of dry ice into your mouth to cool off.

294. ❖ Borrow the smoke detector batteries for your radio.

295. ❖ Use a match to see better when looking for a gas leak on a propane grill.

296. ❖ Answer the phone on the day you know an acquaintance needs help moving.

297. ❖ Joke with the airport security guards about hijacking the plane to Cuba.

298. ❖ Let your parrot who's learning to talk listen to "Beavis and Butthead."

299. ❖ Buy a piano for your third-floor apartment.

300. ❖ Leave a tube of contraceptive cream on the sink next to the tooth-paste.

301. ❖ Hand-feed marshmallows to an alligator.

302. ❖ Ask Grandma to buy you clothes for Christmas.

303. ❖ Use a wastepaper basket as an ashtray.

304. ❖ Brag about having the high score on a game that's on the computer at work.

305. ❖ Lend money to a friend or relative and tell them "Pay me back when you can."

306. ❖ Wear a "Beverly Hills 90210" hat to the shooting range.

307. ❖ Decide to become a vegetarian the day before Thanksgiving.

308. ❖ Park in a tow-away zone for just one minute so that you can run into the store to buy cigarettes.

309. ❖ Store organic fertilized eggs in a basket on the kitchen counter instead of in the refrigerator.

310. ❖ Send the kiddies out to play with the neighbor's guard dog.

311. ❖ Install white carpeting in your house.

312. ❖ Ignore the lightning and continue to play the last few rounds of golf.

313. ❖ Disregarding the advice of those who know him, stay in a damaging relationship certain that your influence will change him.

314. ❖ Steer your little boat closer to Niagara Falls to get a better view.

315. ❖ Attempt to get into the Guinness Book of World Records.

316. ❖ Mail yourself as freight to avoid paying airfare.

317. ❖ Go surfing in hurricane weather to experience the ultimate wave.

318. ❖ Let someone talk you into going to a health farm for that well-earned vacation.

319. ❖ Ignore warning signs because you think they're just for stupid people.

320. ❖ Be in charge of the map and directions for the driver on a long trip.

321. ❖ Take a road that looks like a short cut when you need to be somewhere on time.

322. ❖ Don't disagree when a spouse says "I really look awful."

323. ❖ Have children so that you will have someone to go grocery shopping with.

324. ❖ Teach your children to be totally honest with you about what they do when you're not around.

325. ❖ Believe in the discretion of a co-worker during the company Christmas party.

326. ❖ Be adventurous in your culinary pursuits while visiting Asia.

327. ❖ Take the family dog with you on a trip to Korea.

328. ❖ Be your own best friend.

329. ❖ Read a book of symptoms for fatal diseases.

330. ❖ Raise Japanese beetles for fun and profit.

331. ❖ Drink to good health from a lead cup.

332. ❖ When you need to make a major life decision, consult the daily horoscope in the local paper.

333. ❖ Wear brown shoes with a grey suit.

334. ❖ Hold your breath until you get what you want.

335. ❖ Go to law school to fulfill your desire to make a positive difference in the world.

336. ❖ Go boldly where no one, for good reason, has gone before.

337. ❖ Remove the mosquito netting from your tent so that you can get a better view of the African night sky.

338. ❖ Actually meet one of your heroes.

339. ❖ Fix your own plumbing and do your own electrical work, because how difficult can it be?

340. ❖ Cross-country ski in Nebraska.

341. ❖ Get the terms "cross-training" and "cross-dressing" mixed up when writing a classified ad.

342. ❖ Raise the stakes and try to bluff even though you know you have a losing hand.

343. ❖ Teach an aggressive watch dog to fetch.

344. ❖ Give in to a wild impulse when choosing the paint color for the exterior of your house.

345. ❖ Buy an alarm clock with unlimited snooze control.

346. ❖ Touch an electric fence to see if it's turned on.

347. ❖ Neglect to use the toilet before driving on to a Los Angeles freeway.

348. ❖ Have a romantic interlude from cooking after having sliced a bag of jalapeno peppers.

349. ❖ Refuse emergency aid because you have on old, ugly underwear.

350. ❖ Lie to a priest about your sins in the confessional because you don't have anything interesting to tell.

351. ❖ Exaggerate your symptoms to a surgeon.

352. ❖ Make love in the woods on a bed of poison ivy.

353. ❖ Use traditional lighted candles on the Christmas tree.

354. ❖ Try hallucinogenic drugs as a way to get through the next board of directors meeting.

355. ❖ Take no food on a camping trip because you plan on catching all the fish you can possibly eat.

356. ❖ Burn your bridges with a former employer because you'll never need them again.